kind

imaginative

W9-CCE-456

# bitty ☆ baby

# has a tea party

by Kirby Larson
& Sue Cornelison

★ American Girl®

Special thanks to Dr. Laurie Zelinger, consultant,
child psychologist, and registered play therapist.
Dr. Zelinger reviewed and helped shape the "For Parents"
section, which was written by editorial staff.

Questions or comments? Call 1-800-845-0005,
visit **americangirl.com,** or write to Customer Service,
American Girl, 8400 Fairway Place, Middleton, WI 53562-0497.

Printed in China
14 15 16 17 18 19 20 21 LEO 10 9 8 7 6 5 4 3 2 1

Series Editorial Development: Jennifer Hirsch & Elizabeth Ansfield
Art Direction and Design: Gretchen Becker
Production: Jeannette Bailey, Judith Lary, Paula Moon, Kristi Tabrizi

Cataloging-in-Publication Data available from the Library of Congress

"Look what Auntie sent me!"
I said. Bitty Baby helped
me open the box.
"It's a tea set!"

We ran to show
Mommy.

"Could we have a tea party?" I asked.

"That sounds like fun," Mommy said.
"It would be nice to invite that new little
girl next door."

"She might not like tea parties," I said.

"You won't know until you ask," said Mommy.

I put the teapot in the center of my play table. Bitty Baby helped set the cups around. "Should we add another chair?" I asked. "In case she brings her doll?"

"She might not like dolls," said Bitty Baby.

Mommy looked in. "Are you ready for me to call the new neighbor?"

"No!" I said. "I mean, we still have to dress up."

After Mommy left,
I looked at Bitty Baby.
"What if the new girl
doesn't like to wear
dresses?"

"Or tiaras?" asked
Bitty Baby.

I nodded. "Or curl
her pinky when she
sips her tea?"

Bitty Baby slumped on the floor. "I think I have a tummy ache."

My tummy felt funny, too. "A story might help us both feel better."

Bitty Baby snuggled close. "I'm ready," she said.

One day, Bitty Baby packed her blanket and snacks and set off to pick flowers. As she was walking along, she tumbled over a strange-looking rock.

"I've never seen a rock with
prickles before," she said.

"They're not prickles," said the rock.
"They're spines."

Bitty Baby
looked around.
"Who said that?"

"Me," answered
the rock.

"I've never met a
talking rock before,"
said Bitty Baby.

"I'm not a rock,"
said the rock. "I'm
a hedgehog."

"Why are you all rolled
up like that?"
Bitty Baby asked.

"Because nobody likes
me. I don't have any
friends," said Hedgehog.

"I'll be your friend." Bitty Baby
plunked down on the grass.

Hedgehog rolled around to look at her.
"We can't be friends if you don't like daisies."

"Daisies are very pretty," said Bitty Baby.

Hedgehog huffed.
"I meant, to eat."

"Oh," said Bitty Baby.
"I don't eat flowers."

"What about worm pudding?" Hedgehog asked.

"I like the pudding part," said Bitty Baby.

"But not the worm part?" Hedgehog huffed again.

Bitty Baby shook her head.
"There must be something
we both like," she said.
"What about bubble baths?
Everyone likes those!"

"I don't like any kind of
baths!" said Hedgehog.

Hedgehog curled up tighter than tight again.
He even closed his eyes. "You see, I told
you we couldn't be friends."

"Wait!" Bitty Baby carefully patted Hedgehog's
back. "Friends don't have to like everything
the same."

Hedgehog opened one eye. "They don't?"

"No, they don't," said Bitty Baby, "as long as they like *some* of the same things." She got out her snack. "Do you like cheesy crackers?"

Hedgehog shook his head.

"How about blankets?" Bitty Baby asked.

Hedgehog snuffled. "I like to burrow under things."

Bitty Baby clapped her hands. "Me, too!"

Hedgehog rolled out of his ball and shook himself from snout to tail. He picked some flowers, and then he burrowed under Bitty Baby's blanket with her.

Bitty Baby ate some crackers. Hedgehog ate some flowers. They were both very happy being friends together. The end.

Bitty Baby smiled.
"Even best friends can like
different things," she said.

"Like us," I said. "I like
purple and you like pink."

"Let's get dressed
for our tea party,"
said Bitty Baby.

Mommy called the new neighbor
and she came right over.

"I've never served tea to a truck before," I said.

"And I've never worn a tiara," said my new friend. "I like two lumps of sugar in my tea."

"So do Bitty Baby and I!"

And, curling our pinkies, we drank up every last drop.

# For Parents

## Making New Friends

Having friends is one of the best ways for your child to learn basic social skills like sharing, taking turns, being respectful, and empathizing with others.

## Friendly Phrases

Teach your child the "language of friendship"—words and phrases that encourage positive social behaviors. Ask her questions such as "May I play with you?" or "Is it my turn?" to show the give-and-take nature of social play. Help her come up with a list of simple words that describe what it means to be a good friend, such as "kind." Then take turns play-acting the words on the list so that she can practice what it means to have—and be—a friend.

## Playdate Prep

When you're hosting a playdate, before the guest arrives ask your daughter what she would like to do with her friend, and invite her to help gather toys, games, and craft materials to share. Talk with her about sharing, but be realistic, too. Help her remove favorite toys that she's not ready to share, and put them out of sight. If she starts hoarding her toys, remind her that her friend will be sharing the toys for only a little while and won't be taking them home with her.

## Help Break the Ice

If your child and her guest are feeling shy at first, suggest an activity they could do together or a toy they could share, such as building blocks—or a tea-party set. Once they become comfortable together, let them play without you hovering. Don't worry if they play side by side instead of playing together. This is called *parallel play*; it is normal up through age three.

## Plan a Snack

Find out if your guest has any food restrictions, and be ready to offer a snack partway through the playdate. Food can also provide a positive distraction if a squabble arises.

## Keep It Short

One to two hours is plenty of time for your little one to enjoy her friend's company. You want to avoid having them end their time together tired and cranky. Let them know their playdate will be ending soon, and encourage cleanup by asking your child to give a tour of the playroom or bedroom to show her guest where each toy goes. To end the playdate on a high note and give them something to look forward to, suggest activities to do the next time they get together.

For more parent tips, visit
**americangirl.com/BittyParents**